My Family is a ZOO

K.A. Gerrard   Emma Dodd

BLOOMSBURY

LONDON OXFORD NEW YORK NEW DELHI SYDNEY

Bloomsbury Publishing, London, Oxford, New York, New Delhi and Sydney

First published in the United States of America in March 2016 by Bloomsbury Publishing Plc
1385 Broadway, New York, New York 10018

This edition first published in Great Britain in March 2016 by Bloomsbury Publishing Plc
50 Bedford Square, London WC1B 3DP

Text copyright © K.A. Gerrard
Illustrations copyright © Emma Dodd
The moral rights of the author/illustrator have been asserted

A CIP catalogue record for this book is available from the British Library

ISBN 978 1 4088 6940 6

Printed in China by Leo Paper Products, Heshan, Guangdong

1 3 5 7 9 10 8 6 4 2

www.bloomsbury.com

BLOOMSBURY is a registered trademark of Bloomsbury Publishing Plc

For Emma, with love and gratitude
— K.A.G.

For Kelly, because you make me laugh,
and a day without laughter is a day wasted
— E.D.

My daddy has an elephant
He got when he was three.
It travels with us everywhere.
It's quite a sight to see!

Me, I have my big brown bear.
Surprise! His name is Teddy.
And whatever the adventure,
He is there, waiting and ready.

Today we're going for a drive,
To where I cannot say.

We should arrive by lunchtime
With some stops along the way.

Meet my sister and the whale
That she swims with in the ocean.
It's big and blue and blubbery
And smells of suntan lotion.

Here comes my older brother
With his purple dinosaur.
They may not *seem* ferocious,
But you should hear them *roar!*

Look! My cousin's kangaroo
Has a switch that makes it hop.
Perhaps the switch is broken . . .
The hopping just won't stop!

There's my uncle and his penguin,
Which he once left on the bus.
It travelled round for months
Before returning home to us.

My auntie owns a monkey
With sticky-outy ears.
She bought it on her holiday.
She just loves her souvenirs!

Grandma's brought her bunny,
Whose coat is bald and worn.
It's been loved and hugged and cuddled
Since the day that she was born.

Grandpa's got his tiger,
Who once slept in their bed,

Till Grandma put her foot down.
Now it lives in Grandpa's shed.

Even Boomer has a puppy
That he carries in his jaws.
And every time he goes to sleep,
He hugs it with his paws.

Now we're all together,
With barely room to spare.
Can't wait to see if Mummy
Likes these brand new polar bears.

We make a strange menagerie
As we pile out two by two.
We're not so much a family –
More a family zoo!

At last we have arrived –
Me, Ted and all the others.
And just why have we come here?

To meet my baby brothers!